Here's what kids have to say to
Mary Pope Osborne, author of
the Magic Tree House series:

I never ever read that much until I read the Magic Tree House books, and after I read your books, I got started on reading. I read more and more....Keep on writing, and I will keep on reading.—Seth L.

I had one of your books and I couldn't put it down!!! I really, really love your books.—Liza F.

I'm really enjoying your Magic Tree House books. They are my favorite books....Today I had to write about three people I want to have come over for dinner. The three people I chose are Thomas Jefferson, Nicolas Cage, and, you guessed it, Mary Pope Osborne.—Will B.

I have read every single book you've written....I love your books so much I would go wacko if you stopped writing your books.—Stephanie Z.

Once I start one [of your books], I never put it down until it is done. Your books make me feel like I am really in the place that Jack and Annie are in. When I read one of your books, I learn so many interesting new facts. Your books are the best!—Eliza D.

Parents and teachers love
Magic Tree House books, too!

I am the mother of four young sons who are thoroughly enjoying the adventures of Jack and Annie! We eagerly await each new release! We also use your books as Christmas and birthday gifts for friends and cousins—a welcome gift for the children and their parents!—C. Anders

We overheard the children in the schoolyard talking and laughing about "special friends." Upon further investigation, those friends turned out to be none other than Jack and Annie. These children have become devoted fans of your books. As parents, it is inspiring to see our children so absorbed in books.
—M. Knepper and P. Contessa

The library soon will have a new addition— something that I have dreamed of for a long time—a real wooden Magic Tree House and a beautiful tree mural to accompany it....There are many Magic Tree House experts in every class. It's wonderful to see their enthusiasm and their eagerness to read the books.—R. Locke

Since we are doing a unit on the solar system I chose <u>Midnight on the Moon</u> (Magic Tree House #8). To my delight, this reading turned out to be the most successful thing I've done this year.
—M. Mishkin

Thank you for providing a series of books for children that are mesmerizing, entertaining, and filled with factual information.
—L. Shlansky

My daughter loves to have me read Magic Tree House stories. She's even been known to sleep with one under her pillow!—E. Becker

What a wonderful series you have created! I have even developed a reading program for my more advanced readers centered around your books. The results have been incredible.
—L. Carpenter

The balance between a sophisticated topic and an easy-to-read book is a hard one to find. Thank you for doing it so well.—A. Doolittle

Dear Readers,

As I've said before, my Magic Tree House books are often inspired by ideas that readers send to me. Well, the idea for this book came from Megan Barber, a reader who entered a Magic Tree House writing contest. I am very grateful to Megan for her thoughtful and creative suggestion.

One reason I love writing this series is that the readers I meet and hear from are always so helpful and supportive. If you could see the world from my point of view, you would see it was filled with wonderful kids, kids just like Jack and Annie who love learning new things and going on daring adventures.

So now get ready for <u>your</u> next daring reading adventure...a journey to the time of the Civil War in America.

All my best,

Mary Pope Osborne

Civil War on Sunday

by Mary Pope Osborne

illustrated by
Sal Murdocca

A STEPPING STONE BOOK™

Random House 🏠 New York

For Megan Elizabeth Barber,
who gave me a great idea

Text copyright © 2000 by Mary Pope Osborne.
Illustrations copyright © 2000 by Sal Murdocca.

All rights reserved under International and Pan-American Copyright Conventions.
Published in the United States by Random House, Inc., New York, and simultane-
ously in Canada by Random House of Canada Limited, Toronto.

www.randomhouse.com/kids
www.randomhouse.com/magictreehouse

Library of Congress Cataloging-in-Publication Data
Osborne, Mary Pope.
Civil War on Sunday / by Mary Pope Osborne ; illustrated by Sal Murdocca.
p. cm. — (Magic tree house ; #21) "A Stepping Stone book."
SUMMARY: Jack and Annie are transported by their magic tree house to the time of
the Civil War, where they meet Clara Barton.
ISBN 0-679-89067-X (trade). — ISBN 0-679-99067-4 (lib. bdg.)
[1. Time travel—Fiction. 2. Magic—Fiction.
3. United States—History—Civil War, 1861–1865—Fiction.
4. Barton, Clara, 1821–1912—Fiction. 5. Tree houses—Fiction.]
I. Murdocca, Sal, ill. II. Title. PZ7.O81167Ci 2000 [Fic]—dc21 99-054072

Printed in the United States of America   May 2000   24 23 22 21

Random House, Inc.   New York, Toronto, London, Sydney, Auckland

RANDOM HOUSE and colophon are registered trademarks and A STEPPING STONE BOOK
and colophon are trademarks of Random House, Inc.

Contents

Civil War on Sunday

Prologue

One summer day in Frog Creek, Pennsylvania, a mysterious tree house appeared in the woods.

Eight-year-old Jack and his seven-year-old sister, Annie, climbed into the tree house. They found that it was filled with books.

Jack and Annie soon discovered that the tree house was magic. It could take them to the places in the books. All they had to do was point to a picture and wish to go there.

Along the way, Jack and Annie discovered

that the tree house belongs to Morgan le Fay. Morgan is a magical librarian of Camelot, the long-ago kingdom of King Arthur. She travels through time and space, gathering books.

In Magic Tree House Books #5–8, Jack and Annie helped free Morgan from a spell. In Books #9–12, they solved four ancient riddles and became Master Librarians.

In Magic Tree House Books #13–16, Jack and Annie had to save four ancient stories from being lost forever.

In Magic Tree House Books #17–20, Jack and Annie freed a mysterious little dog from a magic spell.

In Magic Tree House Books #21–24, Jack and Annie have a new challenge. They must find four special kinds of writing for Morgan's library to help save Camelot. They are about to set off to find the first of these…

1

A Light in the Woods

Jack looked out his window.

It was a dreary Sunday afternoon. There were dark clouds in the sky.

Thunder rumbled in the distance.

Jack stared down the street at the Frog Creek woods.

When is the magic tree house coming back? he wondered.

"Hey, guess what!" Annie said. She charged into Jack's room. "I saw a light flash in the woods!"

"It was just lightning," said Jack.

"No, it was magic! A swirl of light!" said Annie. "I think the tree house just came back!"

"I'm sure it was just lightning," Jack said. "Didn't you hear the thunder?"

"Yeah," said Annie. "But let's go check anyway."

She started out of Jack's room. Then she peeked back in.

"Bring your backpack, just in case!" she said.

Jack was always glad for a chance to look for the magic tree house. He grabbed his backpack and followed Annie down the stairs.

"Where are you two going?" their mom called.

"Out to play," said Annie.

"Don't go far," said their mom. "And come in if it starts to rain."

"We will," said Jack. "Don't worry."

They slipped out the front door. Then they ran up the street and into the Frog Creek woods.

The woods were dark under the storm clouds. A cool wind shook the leaves.

Soon Jack and Annie came to the tallest oak tree.

"Oh, man," said Jack. "You were right!"

The magic tree house stood out against the gray sky.

"Morgan!" called Annie.

There was no sign of the enchantress.

"Let's go up!" said Jack.

He grabbed the rope ladder and started up. Annie followed.

They climbed into the tree house. It was hard to see in the dim light.

"Look," said Annie.

She pointed to a piece of paper and a book lying on the floor.

Jack picked up the paper. Annie picked up the book.

"Listen," said Jack. He held the paper close to the window and read aloud:

Dear Jack and Annie,

Camelot is in trouble. To save the kingdom, please find these four special kinds of writing for my library:

Something to follow
Something to send
Something to learn
Something to lend

Thank you,
Morgan

6

"Camelot is in trouble?" said Jack. "What's that mean?"

"I don't know," said Annie. "But we better hurry and find these writings. Let's go look for the first: *Something to follow*."

"I wonder where we should look for it," said Jack. "What's the title of the book you're holding?"

Annie held the book close to the window to read the title.

"Yikes," she said softly. She showed the book to Jack.

On the cover was a painting of a peaceful-looking field and a blue sky. The title said *The Civil War*.

"The Civil War?" said Jack. "Cool."

Annie frowned.

"*Cool?*" she said. "War's not cool."

"It sort of is," Jack said uncomfortably. He knew war was bad. But some parts of it seemed fun, like a game.

"I guess we'll find out," said Annie. She pointed at the cover. "I wish we could go there."

Thunder boomed through the woods.

The wind started to blow.

The tree house started to spin.

It spun faster and faster.

Then everything was still.

Absolutely still.

2

Cruel War

Glaring sunlight filled the tree house.

"It's really hot here," said Jack.

"Especially in these clothes," said Annie.

Their clothes had magically been changed. Annie wore a long dress. Jack wore scratchy pants and a long-sleeved shirt. His backpack was now a leather knapsack.

"Where are we?" asked Annie.

They looked out the window together.

The tree house had landed in a tree at the

10

edge of a field—the same field on the cover of the book.

"It looks so peaceful," said Jack. "Where's the Civil War?"

"There," whispered Annie with a shiver. She pointed to the woods beyond the field.

Jack saw a soldier riding a horse out of the woods. The horse was covered with mud. The soldier's blue uniform was torn. His arm was bloody.

Another man rode into the field. His blue uniform was in rags, too. His head was bandaged.

"Oh, man," whispered Jack. "Who are they?"

He opened the Civil War book and found a painting of some soldiers in blue. He read to Annie:

1861–1865
The Civil War is also called the "War
Between the States," because it was
fought between the Southern and
Northern states of the United States.
Southerners wore gray uniforms and
were called *Confederate soldiers.*
Northerners wore blue uniforms and
were called *Union soldiers.*

"So they're Union soldiers," said Jack. He pulled out his notebook and wrote:

Civil War—1861–1865
Blue = North = Union
Gray = South = Confederate

Jack looked at his book again. He read aloud:

The Civil War was a cruel and bloody

**war. More people died in this war
than in all of America's other wars
put together. One out of every five
young men in the nation died or was
wounded.**

"That's so sad," said Annie.

Jack wrote in his notebook:

cruel war

"Wow, they keep coming," Annie said.

Jack looked up. More Union soldiers were coming through the field. These didn't have horses.

They all looked sad and weary. Some of them limped. Some of them helped others along. One man stumbled and fell down.

"I have to help—" said Annie.

"Wait!" said Jack.

She started down the rope ladder.

"You can't help!" said Jack. "A kid can't help…"

But Annie kept going.

"Don't forget—we have to find some special writing for Morgan!" Jack called in a loud whisper. *"Something to follow!"*

He packed the Civil War book and his notebook in his knapsack. Then he started down the ladder.

When he stepped onto the ground, Jack saw Annie in the distance.

She was holding her hand out to the fallen soldier. She helped him to his feet.

The soldier slowly started walking again. Annie walked beside him.

"Oh, brother," said Jack. And he hurried to catch up with Annie.

The sun was scorching hot as Jack ran through the dry field. He was sweaty in his scratchy clothes.

He caught up with Annie. Together, they walked silently with the soldiers.

At the edge of the field was a steep hill. Everyone stopped and gazed at the sight below them—rows and rows of white tents.

"Thank goodness," said the soldier beside Jack. "We're saved."

3

Field Hospital

Jack and Annie walked with the soldiers into the camp.

Outside one tent was a long line of men in torn blue uniforms. They looked tired and hurt. Many were bloody and barely able to stand.

Women wearing dark dresses were giving out food and water to the men in line.

"Where are we?" asked Annie.

"I'll find out," said Jack.

He pulled out their book and found a picture of the campsite. He read:

> During the Civil War, *field hospitals*
> were set up quickly near battlefields to
> treat wounded soldiers. Soldiers stayed
> in the field hospitals for a short time
> before going back to fight, or moving to a
> larger hospital, or being sent home. This
> field hospital in Virginia took care of
> over 400 patients.

"That's a lot," said Annie.

"It sure is," said Jack.

He pulled out his notebook and wrote:

field hospital—set up near battlefield

Jack read aloud again from the book:

> More than 3,000 women helped out as
> nurses during the Civil War. Nursing

was a new job for women in America.
Before the war, only men had been
nurses.

"Wow," said Annie. "Maybe *we* can be nurses."

"Forget it," said Jack. "Kids can't be nurses."

Jack wanted to find the special writing for Morgan and go home. The sad scene at the field hospital was making him feel sick.

"I'll just ask," said Annie.

She headed over to a nurse cooking over a campfire.

"Annie! We've got a mission!" Jack called.

But Annie kept going.

Jack heaved a sigh. He tucked his note-book and the Civil War book under his arm and followed her.

Waves of heat rose from a small cooking

fire. The young nurse was heating a pot of coffee.

Flies buzzed everywhere.

"Hello," said Annie.

The nurse barely smiled at them.

Her face was red and beaded with sweat. Her eyes looked terribly tired.

"Where are you from?" she asked.

"Frog Creek," said Annie. "We'd like to volunteer as nurses."

The young woman didn't seem at all surprised.

"We could certainly use some help," she said, sighing. "Some of us have not slept for days."

"Why not?" asked Jack.

"The wounded are coming here from a battle near Richmond," said the nurse. "More and more keep coming. It never seems to end."

"Just tell us what to do," said Annie.

"While we feed the new patients, you can go to the first two tents," the young nurse said, "and give the other soldiers their noon meal."

She pointed to a basket filled with bread and potatoes. Next to it was a ladle and a bucket filled with water.

"Anything else?" Annie asked.

"Just try to give them comfort," the nurse said.

"How do we do that?" said Annie.

"I don't have time to show you," the nurse said. "But here's a list of things that can help."

She pulled a piece of paper from her apron pocket and handed it to Annie.

Annie read the list to Jack:

> Be cheerful.
> Lessen sorrow and give hope.
> Be brave.
> Put aside your own feelings.
> Don't give up.

"Follow that list," said the nurse, "and you can't go wrong."

The nurse took the pot of coffee from the fire and carried it to the line of men.

"Follow…" said Jack. *"Follow that list…"*

"That's what she said," said Annie.

Jack took the list from her.

"Don't you get it?" he said. *"This is it!* We found it! The special writing for Morgan's library! *Something to follow."*

"Yes!" said Annie.

Jack put the paper into his knapsack.

"It was handed right to us!" he said, smiling. "We can go home now!"

"Oh, no! Not now!" said Annie. "We have to help as nurses first."

"But, Annie—" said Jack.

She picked up the food basket. Then she

started toward the row of white tents.

"Wait—we're supposed to leave," Jack said weakly. "Our mission is over."

The truth was that he didn't want to help. He didn't want to be around wounded and suffering soldiers. It was too sad.

"Bring the water bucket and the ladle!" Annie shouted. Then she disappeared inside the first tent.

Jack groaned. He knew he couldn't change her mind.

He pulled out the list and read the first line: *Be cheerful.*

"Oh, brother," he said.

Jack put the list back into his knapsack. He picked up the heavy bucket. Hurrying clumsily after Annie, he tried to smile.

4

Freedom Fighters

Jack carried the water bucket into the tent.

The scene inside was like a nightmare.

The tent was hot and stuffy. A dozen injured soldiers lay on small cots. Some called for food. Others begged for water or just moaned.

Jack wanted to rush back outside. But Annie got right to work. She rolled up her sleeves and smiled.

"Hi, everybody!" she said cheerfully.

None of the soldiers smiled back.

"I have good news!" she said. "We've brought lunch!"

Annie moved down the row of cots. She handed out pieces of bread and chunks of potatoes to all the patients.

"You'll be feeling better soon," she said to one sick man. "You'll see your family again," she told another.

Jack looked around nervously. He wasn't sure what to do.

"Give them water, Jack!" Annie called to him.

Jack saw a tin cup beside each man's cot. He picked up the first cup. Carefully, he used the ladle to fill it with water.

Keeping his eyes down, Jack handed the cup to the patient. He felt shy and uncomfortable. He didn't know what to say.

Jack moved on to the next patient, then the next. He gave each wounded man a cup of water. But he never looked right at any of them or spoke a word.

Soon Jack and Annie had finished passing out food and water.

"Good-bye!" Annie said.

She waved and left the tent. Jack quickly followed her.

"Let's go home now," he begged once they were outside. "We've got what we came for."

"If we leave now, the patients in the next tent will go hungry and thirsty," said Annie.

Jack sighed.

"Okay," he said. "But after we take care of them, we're leaving for sure."

He followed Annie into the next tent.

Just like the last tent, it was filled with wounded soldiers. But the soldiers in this tent were all African-Americans.

"Hi, everybody!" Annie said, smiling warmly.

Again, she passed out potatoes and bread. She also talked and made jokes.

Jack poured water into each of the tin cups. Again, he didn't speak to any of the soldiers. But as he handed over the last cup, a patient spoke to him.

"Thank you for your kindness, son," the soldier said.

Jack glanced shyly at the man on the cot. He was an elderly, silver-haired black man.

"You're welcome," said Jack.

He tried to think of something else to say. He remembered Annie's cheerful words.

"You'll get well soon," he told the patient. "You'll be with your family again."

The man shook his head.

"No. I'll never be with my family again," he said quietly. "My wife and children were sold long ago."

"Sold?" said Jack.

"Yes. We were slaves," the man said.

"*You* were a slave?" asked Jack.

"All of us in this tent were once slaves," the man said. "We ran away from our owners in the South to fight to end slavery, to fight for freedom for our people. I ran barefoot for over thirty miles to tell the Union soldiers that the Confederates were going to attack."

The man fell silent.

"You're a very brave freedom fighter," said Jack.

"Thank you, son." The man closed his eyes.

Jack wanted to know more about slavery. But he didn't want to bother the weary patient. He pulled out the Civil War book.

He found a picture of African-Americans standing on a platform. The men, women, and children had chains on their hands and feet.

Jack read:

> In the 1800s, the United States was
> divided over the issue of slavery. The
> North wanted the country to end all
> slavery. But the South wanted to keep
> slaves because more than four million
> African-American slaves worked in
> the huge plantation fields there. This
> disagreement between the North and
> South led to the Civil War.

Jack looked down at the man's face. He looked very weary.

Jack pulled the nurse's list of rules from his knapsack.

Lessen sorrow and give hope, he read.

Jack put the list away. He leaned close to the man and spoke in a soft voice: "One day your great-great-grandchildren will be doctors and lawyers," he said.

The man opened his eyes.

Jack went on. "They'll help run the government and schools. They'll be senators and generals and teachers and principals."

The man stared hard into Jack's eyes.

"Can you see the future, son?" he asked.

Jack nodded. "In a way…" he said.

The man smiled a beautiful smile.

"Thank you, son," he said. Then he closed his eyes again.

"Good luck," whispered Jack. He hoped the brave man would live to enjoy freedom.

"Ready to go home now, Jack?" said Annie. She had finished passing out the food.

Jack nodded.

As he and Annie stepped out of the tent,

they heard someone shout, "She's back!"

A horse-drawn wagon was barreling into the camp.

"Who's back?" asked Annie.

"Clara Barton," a patient said. "She runs this hospital."

"*Clara Barton!*" said Annie. "I don't believe it!"

"Who's Clara Barton?" asked Jack. He'd heard the name before. But he couldn't remember who she was.

"Who's Clara Barton?" said Annie. "Are you nuts?"

She ran to meet the wagon.

5

Angel of the Battlefield

Jack still didn't remember who Clara Barton was. He pulled out the Civil War book and read:

Clara Barton was a famous Civil War nurse. When she began nursing, she used her own money for her supplies. She drove a horse-drawn "ambulance" right onto the battlefield to help save wounded soldiers. For this reason she became known as the "Angel of the Battlefield."

Jack put the book away. Then he hurried to Annie.

He looked at the woman sitting in the driver's seat of the wagon.

She doesn't look like an angel, Jack thought.

The woman was very small. She had a plain, serious face and dark hair pulled back in a bun. She wore a long black skirt and a black jacket.

In the back of her wagon were more wounded soldiers in torn, bloody uniforms. They moaned and cried out.

Nurses, both men and women, were putting the wounded men on stretchers.

Clara Barton wiped her forehead. She looked hot and tired.

"Can we help you, Miss Barton?" Annie asked.

"Who are you?" said Clara Barton.

"Jack and Annie," said Annie. "We're volunteer nurses. What can we do, Miss Barton?"

Clara Barton smiled.

"First, you can call me Clara," she said. "Second, would you ride with me back toward the battlefield? There are more wounded waiting to be picked up."

"Sure!" said Annie.

Jack didn't answer. After seeing all the suffering men in the wagon, he was afraid of getting closer to the battlefield.

"And you?" Clara asked Jack. Her dark, serious eyes looked right into his.

Jack didn't want to admit he was afraid. "Sure, no problem," he said.

"Very good," said Clara Barton. "Let's go."

Jack and Annie climbed up into the driver's seat next to her.

By now, all the soldiers had been taken out of the wagon.

"Take care of my new family members," Clara called to the nurses.

She snapped the reins. The horse-drawn ambulance rolled off, sending up clouds of dust.

6

Keep Low!

The wagon jerked and swayed as it bumped over the dry ground.

Jack felt as though he were frying in the hot sunlight. Dust from the road filled his throat and eyes.

The boom of cannons grew louder and louder. Jack heard popping sounds, too, like the noise of firecrackers.

"What's that popping noise?" he shouted, blinded by the dust and sunlight.

"Musket fire!" said Clara.

Jack remembered that muskets were long, old-fashioned guns.

"What are those flashes?" asked Annie.

Jack tried to open his eyes and see what she was talking about.

He saw bright flashes of light in the distance and puffs of smoke in the sky.

"Cannon shells exploding," said Clara Barton. "Shells are like small bombs. They have ruined much farmland."

Jack squinted at the passing countryside. The ground was filled with ugly holes. Long ditches were also cut through the fields.

"Did the shells make those ditches, too?" he asked.

"No. Those are trenches the soldiers dug for a battle," Clara said. "Each side digs their own. Day after day, they sit in the trenches, firing their muskets at one another."

Jack tried to imagine how terrible it would be to sit in a trench all day, waiting to be shot—or waiting to shoot someone else.

"We have to get some water," said Clara.

She drove the wagon to a narrow creek. A stream of water flowed downhill, running over rocks.

The wagon came to a halt. Jack heard a whistling sound, then another.

"Keep low!" cried Clara.

"What's that?" Jack asked.

"Cannon fire!" she said.

Jack and Annie crouched down in the driver's seat.

Jack felt a rush of panic. He pulled out their list. His hands were shaking as he read:

Be brave.

Oh, great, he thought.

Another cannon shell whizzed overhead, then another.

The ground exploded over and over in flashes of light. Dirt clods flew everywhere. Clouds of smoke and more dust filled the air.

The horses neighed and whinnied.

Be brave! Jack thought. *Be brave!*

7

Helping Hands

The firing came to an end. The horses calmed down. The smoky air began to clear.

Clara handed Jack and Annie each a canteen.

"Fill these quickly," she said. "We have no time to waste."

Jack's legs felt wobbly as he followed Annie to the creek. They filled their canteens, then climbed back into the wagon.

"Keep alert," said Clara. "Look for the

46

wounded as they come off the battlefield."

She snapped the reins. The horses started off again.

As they bumped along, Jack looked ahead for wounded soldiers.

"There!" said Annie.

She pointed to a man limping toward them and waving his arms.

The man looked very young, more like a teenage boy. His uniform was torn and bloody. It wasn't a blue uniform, though. It was gray.

Clara pulled the horses to a stop.

"But he's a *Confederate* soldier," said Jack.

"When someone is hurt, you give them a helping hand, no matter who they are," said Clara. Her voice got softer. "I have seen courage and kindness on both sides of this war. Sometimes things are not as simple as they seem."

Jack was glad they had stopped to help the soldier.

He jumped out of the wagon.

"Do you need a helping hand?" he asked the young man.

"Thank you," the soldier said softly.

Jack helped him into the back of the wagon. The soldier lay down on a pile of blankets and closed his eyes.

Jack climbed back onto the seat beside Clara. She snapped the reins, and they rode on.

They came across more ragged men resting in the shade of an oak tree. These soldiers all wore blue uniforms.

Again, Clara stopped the horses.

"See if any of those men need a ride to the hospital," she said to Jack and Annie.

Jack glanced at the soldier sleeping in the back of the wagon.

"Can a Confederate and a Union soldier be together?" he asked worriedly.

Clara nodded.

"Sometimes men are simply too sick and tired to be enemies anymore," she said. "Sometimes they even know each other. Many families and friendships have been torn apart by this war."

"Let's go," said Annie, hopping out of the wagon. Jack followed her.

They carried their canteens to the men under the oak tree.

"Hi!" said Annie. "Does anyone need to go to the hospital?"

"Only John, our drummer boy," a soldier said. "He's suffering from heat stroke. But we all need some water, miss."

Jack saw a young boy lying on the ground. His eyes were closed.

"Oh, Jack!" whispered Annie. "He looks just like *you*."

The boy *did* look a lot like Jack—just a few years older.

"We better get him to Clara's ambulance right away," Annie said.

She handed her canteen to one of the tired soldiers. Another soldier lifted the drummer boy to his feet.

The boy opened his eyes and mumbled a few words. He tried to walk, but he swayed as if he were about to faint.

"Wait—" Jack grabbed the boy. "We'll give

you a helping hand," he said.

The drummer boy put his arms around Jack's and Annie's shoulders.

"Just a little further, John," Annie said. "You're doing great. Just a little further..."

The drummer boy moved as if he were walking in his sleep. His head hung down. His feet shuffled in the dust.

"Take good care of him!" one of the men called. "We can't do without him!"

8

Brothers

Clara Barton had turned the wagon around. She helped Jack and Annie lift the drummer boy into the back.

"The soldiers said he has heat stroke," Annie told Clara. "His name is John."

The boy lay down next to the sleeping Confederate soldier.

"He does have heat stroke," Clara said. "The other boy also has a high fever. We must get them to the hospital at once. Can you two stay in the back of the wagon and do as I tell you?"

"Sure," said Jack and Annie.

Clara dampened two clean cloths with water from Jack's canteen.

"Gently press these cloths against their faces to help cool them off," she said.

She gave the cloths to Jack and Annie.

Then she went to the front of the wagon and climbed in. The wagon started forward.

Jack and Annie gently patted the soldiers' faces with the damp cloths. Jack looked at the young men lying side by side. The two seemed far more alike than different.

In another time and place, they might have been friends, Jack thought.

Finally, the wagon arrived at the field hospital. The Confederate soldier was put on a stretcher and carried to a tent.

Two soldiers wearing bandages put the drummer boy on a stretcher.

"Could you stay with John awhile?" Clara Barton asked Jack and Annie.

"Sure," said Jack.

"Try to bring down his fever," Clara said. "A nurse will give you ice packs to press against his skin. Find me when his fever is lower."

The drummer boy was carried into an empty tent. Jack and Annie followed.

John was put on a cot. Then a nurse brought some rags and a bucket filled with ice. Jack and Annie were left alone with the boy.

Jack wrapped some ice in a rag. He pressed the ice pack against the boy's head and neck and arms. Annie fanned the air to cool John off and to keep away the flies.

Jack felt so hot he pressed an ice pack against his own face for a moment. Then he looked up *drummer boys* in his Civil War book. He read:

> The Civil War was the last war to use drummer boys. The drumbeat was used to give orders to soldiers. Different beats told them when to eat, how to march, and even how to fight. On smoky battlefields, the boy's drumming helped soldiers find one another and keep together.

"Wow," said Jack. He closed the book, pulled out his notebook, and wrote:

drummer boy—really important job

Suddenly, John shouted. Jack looked up from his notebook. The drummer boy was still asleep, but he was waving his arms as if he were having a nightmare.

Annie shook the boy's arm.

"Wake up, John," she said. "You're okay. Wake up."

The drummer boy opened his eyes.

"You were having a bad dream," said Annie. "You're safe now. You'll see your family again soon."

"No! No!" the boy said. He sounded frantic. "I have to go back to the battlefield."

"No, you don't have to fight anymore," said Annie. "You can go home and be safe."

"No!" the boy said. "They need me! They need my drum!" He sounded more and more upset.

Jack thought about their list.

Put aside your own feelings, he remembered.

"Okay, John," said Jack. "You can go back as soon as you feel better."

"Jack!" said Annie. "He'll get hurt or killed! I'm afraid for him!"

"Me too," Jack said softly. "But we have to put our own feelings aside. That's one of the things on our list."

Annie sighed.

"Okay," she said sadly. She looked at John. "If you want to fight again in the Civil War, you can. If that's what you really want."

"Thank you," the boy whispered.

"You know, you're the bravest kid I've ever met," Jack said.

The drummer boy smiled at Jack.

"You look just like my little brother," he said hoarsely.

"You look just like my *big* brother," said Jack, "except I don't have a big brother. I don't have any brothers."

The three of them laughed. The drummer boy's laugh was very soft.

The boy laid his head back on his pillow and closed his eyes again.

In a moment, he was sleeping peacefully. A smile was on his lips.

Annie felt his forehead.

"His fever's gone down," she said. "We should go tell Clara."

Annie left the tent.

Jack got up and slowly followed her.

When he reached the entrance of the tent,

he turned and looked back. The shadows of twilight fell across the boy's calm, sleeping face.

It was strange. Jack hardly knew the drummer boy. But he felt they *could* be brothers.

Listening to the cannon fire in the distance, Jack was afraid for the boy.

Will he live to see his family again? Jack wondered.

"Good luck, John," Jack said softly.

With a heavy heart, Jack stepped out into the warm evening air.

9

Don't Give Up

"Annie?" said Jack.

"Over here!" she called.

Jack saw two figures standing in the twilight.

He walked over to Annie and Clara. They all stared in the direction of the distant battlefield.

Bright lights flashed against the dark blue horizon—cannon shells exploding.

"Every time you see a flash, you know a

shell may have taken a life or many lives," said Clara.

"That's awful," said Annie.

"Yes, it is," said Clara. "A whole world can vanish in that flash—all a young man's joys and sorrows, all his memories."

"This *is* a cruel war!" said Annie.

"All wars are cruel," said Clara Barton. "People feel they must fight for causes they believe in. But they soon discover that war is not about glory and fame. It's about misery and terrible pain and sadness."

"It makes me miss my mom and dad," said Annie. "It makes me *really* miss them."

Annie sounded tired and homesick. Finally, she had lost her cheerfulness.

"I think it's time for you two to go home," said Clara.

Jack thought of all the wounded men who needed food and water and kindness and comfort.

"No!" Jack said. "We have to stay. We can't give up. That's on the list—*Don't give up.*"

Jack pulled out their list to show Clara Barton.

"Oh, yes," she said, nodding. "I see one of my nurses has written down the things I often say. Let me add one thing more—*Do not forget the ones who love you.*"

Jack heaved a big sigh. He was homesick, too.

"Can we keep the list?" he asked.

"Of course," said Clara. "You don't have to work in a hospital to follow my words. They work in all of life no matter where you go."

"Thanks," said Jack.

64

"My thanks to both of you," said Clara Barton. "You were great helpers."

"You were a great teacher," said Annie.

"Good-bye," said Clara Barton. "Be very careful going home."

"We will," said Jack and Annie. "Bye."

The sun was setting as they walked out of the camp. The boom of cannons sounded in the distance.

Soldiers sang a song around a campfire.

> *We're tenting tonight*
> *   on the old camp ground;*
> *Give us a song to cheer*
> *Our weary hearts,*
> *   a song of home,*
> *And friends we love so dear.*

Jack and Annie walked through the darkening field. By the time they reached the woods, the stars were out.

They climbed up the rope ladder to the tree house. Annie grabbed the Pennsylvania book.

"Wait," said Jack.

He looked out the window. He couldn't see anything below. But the soldiers' song still carried through the warm, starry night.

> *Many are the hearts*
> *that are weary tonight,*
> *Wishing for the war to cease...*

As Jack listened, he thought of Clara Barton, the elderly slave, the young Confederate soldier, and John, the drummer boy...

"War is not a game," Jack said softly. "It is definitely not a game."

Many are the hearts
    looking for the right
    To see the dawn of peace.

The song ended. The cannon fire stopped. The night was quiet, except for the croaking of frogs.

"Ready?" Annie whispered.

"Ready," said Jack.

"I *really* wish we could go home," Annie said, pointing to the picture of the Frog Creek woods.

The wind started to blow.

The tree house started to spin.

It spun faster and faster.

Then everything was still.

Absolutely still.

10

Home, Sweet Home

There was a booming in the distance.

Jack opened his eyes and caught his breath. *Is that cannon fire?* he wondered. *Are we still back in the Civil War?*

"We're home," said Annie. "Home, sweet home."

"Oh, man," Jack whispered.

They *were* home. They were back in the Frog Creek woods. They were wearing their own comfortable clothes again.

The cannon fire was really only thunder. At that moment, Jack loved the thunder.

Raindrops tapped against the tree house.

"We better hurry," said Jack.

"Wait. Leave the list in the tree house," said Annie. "It's the first special writing for Morgan's library. *Something to follow.*"

Jack took the list of Clara Barton's rules out of his pack. He put it on the floor next to Morgan's letter.

"I wonder how that list will help save Camelot?" he said.

"I don't know," said Annie. "But you know what's weird about getting that list? I think we couldn't just have taken it home when we first got it. We had to *live* it first."

Jack nodded. Annie was completely right, he thought. He picked up his backpack.

"Wait! I see another note!" said Annie.

She picked a piece of paper off the tree-house floor. On it was written: *Come back on Wednesday.*

"I guess that's when Morgan wants us to look for the next special writing," said Annie.

"That's in three days," said Jack. "Let's go home and rest."

He started down the rope ladder. Annie followed.

When they stepped onto the ground, the rain began to pour down.

"Run!" said Jack.

They ran through the Frog Creek woods, then down their street. They ran to their porch and dashed into their dry, cozy house.

They found their parents reading in the living room.

"Dad! Mom!" Annie cried. "We're so glad to see you!"

"Well, we're—we're glad to see you, too," their dad said, sounding a little puzzled.

"Go put on dry clothes," said their mom.

Jack and Annie started up to their rooms. Halfway up the stairs, Jack stopped.

"Oh, I have a question," he called to his parents. "Did anyone in our family fight in the Civil War?"

Their dad looked surprised. "Yes," he said. "One of your great-great-great-grandfathers was a drummer boy."

"Oh, man," whispered Jack.

"What was his name, Dad?" asked Annie.

"John," their dad said.

Jack and Annie gasped.

"And—and what happened to John?" Jack asked. "Was he hurt in the war?"

"No, he grew up to be a schoolteacher," their mom said. "He had five children."

Jack and Annie whooped with joy.

"That's great news!" said Annie.

"*Really* great news!" said Jack. "Thanks for telling us!"

"Sure." Their dad smiled, though he looked puzzled again.

As Jack hurried up to his room, some words from the Civil War song ran through his mind:

> *Give us a song to cheer*
> *Our weary hearts, a song of home...*

FACTS FOR YOU AND JACK

1) More soldiers were killed in the Civil War than in any other war in American history.

2) In 1861, when the Civil War began, about 3½ million people were slaves in the South.

3) In 1865, President Abraham Lincoln convinced Congress to pass the 13th Amendment to the Constitution, which abolished slavery throughout the nation.

4) Eleven states fought for the Confederacy. Twenty-three states fought for the Union. A number of territories also fought for the Union.

5) Soldiers during the Civil War often sang songs together. One of the most famous songs was "Tenting Tonight on the Old Camp Ground," written in 1861 by Walter Kittredge.

"Tenting Tonight on the Old Camp Ground"

We're tenting tonight on the old camp ground;
Give us a song to cheer
Our weary hearts, a song of home,
And friends we love so dear.

(Chorus)
Many are the hearts that are weary tonight,
Wishing for the war to cease;
Many are the hearts looking for the right
To see the dawn of peace.
Tenting tonight, tenting tonight,
Tenting on the old camp ground.

We've been tenting tonight on the old
 camp ground,
Thinking of days gone by,
Of the loved ones at home that gave us the hand
And the tear that said, "Good-bye!"

(Chorus)

Check out the Website *www.civilwarmusic.net/songs.html* for
more songs of the Civil War.

CLARA BARTON

Clara Barton, known as the "Angel of the Battle-field," nursed soldiers during the Civil War. She also used her own money to bring them supplies. After the war, she formed a bureau to search for soldiers who were missing as a result of the war. Her work brought information to more than 22,000 families.

In 1881, Clara Barton founded the American Red Cross. Her organization not only provides relief during times of war but also helps people who have suffered terrible natural disasters, such as hurricanes or floods.

DRUMMER BOYS

It is thought that nearly 60,000 boys served as drummer boys or buglers in the Civil War. One of the youngest drummer boys was Johnny Clem, who enlisted at the age of eleven. He was so brave that he was made a sergeant when he was only thirteen!

339

MAGIC TREE HOUSE®

Ciao, amici!

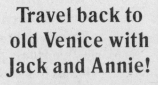

Travel back to old Venice with Jack and Annie!

Merlin has asked Jack and Annie to help on another magical mission! This time they travel back to Venice, Italy. With the help of some new friends, a special book, and a mysterious rhyme from Merlin, the heroes just might save the beautiful city from a gigantic flood!

195

Where have you traveled in the

MAGIC TREE HOUSE?

The Mystery of the Tree House
(Books #1–4)

❏ **Magic Tree House #1, Dinosaurs Before Dark,** in which Jack and Annie discover the tree house and travel back to the time of dinosaurs.

❏ **Magic Tree House #2, The Knight at Dawn,** in which Jack and Annie go to the time of knights and explore a medieval castle with a hidden passage.

❏ **Magic Tree House #3, Mummies in the Morning,** in which Jack and Annie go to ancient Egypt and get lost in a pyramid when they help a ghost queen.

❏ **Magic Tree House #4, Pirates Past Noon,** in which Jack and Annie travel back in time and meet some unfriendly pirates searching for buried treasure.

The Mystery of the Magic Spell
(Books #5–8)

❏ **Magic Tree House #5, Night of the Ninjas,** in which Jack and Annie go to old Japan and learn the secrets of the ninjas.

❏ **Magic Tree House #6, Afternoon on the Amazon,** in which Jack and Annie explore the wild rain forest of the Amazon and are greeted by army ants, crocodiles, and flesh-eating piranhas.

❏ **Magic Tree House #7, Sunset of the Sabertooth,** in which Jack and Annie go back to the Ice Age—the world of woolly mammoths, sabertooth tigers, and a mysterious sorcerer.

❏ **Magic Tree House #8, Midnight on the Moon,** in which Jack and Annie go forward in time and explore the moon in a moon buggy.

The Mystery of the Ancient Riddles
(Books #9–12)

❑ **Magic Tree House #9, Dolphins at Daybreak,** in which Jack and Annie arrive on a coral reef, where they find a mini-submarine that takes them underwater into the world of sharks and dolphins.

❑ **Magic Tree House #10, Ghost Town at Sundown,** in which Jack and Annie travel to the Wild West, where they battle horse thieves, meet a kindly cowboy, and get some help from a mysterious ghost.

❑ **Magic Tree House #11, Lions at Lunchtime,** in which Jack and Annie go to the plains of Africa, where they help wild animals cross a rushing river and have a picnic with a Masai warrior.

❑ **Magic Tree House #12, Polar Bears Past Bedtime,** in which Jack and Annie go to the Arctic, where they get help from a seal hunter, play with polar bear cubs, and get trapped on thin ice.

The Mystery of the Lost Stories
(Books #13–16)

❑ **Magic Tree House #13, VACATION ON THE VOLCANO,** in which Jack and Annie land in Pompeii during Roman times, on the very day Mount Vesuvius erupts!

❑ **Magic Tree House #14, DAY OF THE DRAGON KING,** in which Jack and Annie travel back to ancient China, where they must face an emperor who burns books.

❑ **Magic Tree House #15, VIKING SHIPS AT SUNRISE,** in which Jack and Annie visit a monastery in medieval Ireland on the day the Vikings attack!

❑ **Magic Tree House #16, HOUR OF THE OLYMPICS,** in which Jack and Annie are whisked back to ancient Greece and the first Olympic games.

The Mystery of the Enchanted Dog
(Books #17–20)

❏ **Magic Tree House #17, Tonight on the Titanic,** in which Jack and Annie travel back to the decks of the *Titanic* and help two children escape from the sinking ship.

❏ **Magic Tree House #18, Buffalo Before Breakfast,** in which Jack and Annie go back in time to the Great Plains, where they meet a Lakota boy and have to stop a buffalo stampede!

❏ **Magic Tree House #19, Tigers at Twilight,** in which Jack and Annie are whisked away to a forest in India...and are stalked by a hungry tiger!

❏ **Magic Tree House #20, Dingoes at Dinnertime,** in which Jack and Annie must help a baby kangaroo and a koala bear escape from a wildfire in an Australian forest.

Look for these other books
by Mary Pope Osborne!

Picture books:
Mo and His Friends
Moonhorse
Rocking Horse Christmas

For middle-grade readers:
Adaline Falling Star
American Tall Tales
The Deadly Power of Medusa
Favorite Greek Myths
Favorite Medieval Tales
Favorite Norse Myths
The Life of Jesus in Masterpieces of Art
Mermaid Tales from Around the World
One World, Many Religions
*Spider Kane and the Mystery Under
    the May-Apple (#1)*
*Spider Kane and the Mystery at
    Jumbo Nightcrawler's (#2)*
Standing in the Light

For young adult readers:
Haunted Waters